Merry Christmas

to: The Van Dalen's

:)

from: The Hutchins

2005

Dedicated to the three best cookie makers I know…
Hope, Ashley and Brooke

The Sweetest Story Ever Told

A NEW CHRISTMAS TRADITION FOR FAMILIES

LYSA TERKEURST

Illustrated by *Michal Sparks*

MOODY PRESS
CHICAGO

Mr. Gifford Bowne
Indigo Gate
1 Pegasus Drive
Colts Neck, NJ 07722
(732) 577-9333

Border Illustrations: Mary Ragont

ISBN 0-8024-7094-7

3 5 7 9 10 8 6 4 2

A special thank you to Helen Miller who passed on this wonderful cookie recipe through Amie Goodman so many years ago.

Peter loved Christmas. He loved the lights that danced and twinkled on the trees. He loved the sounds of carolers proclaiming a holy birth and bells ringing in the season. He especially loved delivering bundles of packages and Christmas cards and watching delighted wide-eyed children shake and examine their treasures. But his favorite Christmas tradition was making his Christmas sugar cookies and telling the sweetest story ever told. Soon it would be time to make his special cookies. Peter could hardly wait.

As he suited up in his crisp blue uniform, he wondered how many packages would be waiting for him today. After kissing his wife, Prissy, he climbed into his red, white, and blue mail truck and headed downtown.

$\mathcal{E}$veryone knew Peter and waved and honked to him as he drove through town. The Simpson sisters waved from their front porch where they were hanging greenery adorned with bright red bows. Mr. Thomas was busy shoveling fresh snow from his walkway but took time to smile and nod. Little Suzy Warner giggled as she jumped up, landed flat on her back, and made a snow angel on the post office lawn.

Peter climbed out of his truck and made his way inside. He smiled as he approached his section of the post office. His mailbags were stuffed full, and brown packages were stacked taller than he was. *The children sure will be happy today,* thought Peter.

As he finished loading his truck, little Suzy ran up and asked if he'd seen any packages addressed to her family. Peter looked at the snow-covered angel-maker and shook his head. "Not today, Suzy, but there is still plenty of time. Check back tomorrow and stay out of that snow before you catch a cold. It's almost Christmas, and you don't want to get sick," Peter said.

Peter watched the little girl smile, turn, and skip toward home. He hoped that there would be packages for the Warners. They were new to town and Peter didn't know much about them. He did know that Mr. Warner was away on business a lot and Mrs. Warner spent her time taking care of their small home on Cottage Lane. He also knew that they rarely got any mail except bills. Peter said a prayer for the Warners asking God to please have someone send little Suzy a special Christmas package.

Abbeville was always
a special little town, but at
Christmas Peter thought it was
the greatest place on earth.
He loved the brick buildings
on Main Street, the colorful
old houses, and most of
all, the wonderful people that called this town "home".

As he made his delivery rounds he prayed for each family. He prayed that Jesus would be the center of all holiday festivities within each home. He prayed over each package that, as the family opened their gifts, they would think about the greatest gift given in that small manger so many years ago.

$\mathcal{S}$ oon he was turning down Cottage Lane and making his way to the Warner home. He decided to deliver Mrs. Warner's mail to her door and save her the trip out in the cold. Mrs. Warner was surprised to see her friendly visitor. He could tell she had been crying. He asked how he might pray for her. She told him money was especially tight this year with the move. She knew Suzy wasn't expecting much but she couldn't stand the thought of giving her nothing at all.

Peter knew after his conversation with Mrs. Warner that it was time to make his cookies. As soon as he finished making his deliveries, he rushed home and told Prissy of his plan.

Prissy called Mrs. Warner to invite her and Suzy over for a special holiday gathering later that day. Mrs. Warner gladly accepted. Prissy then called several other families and before long Peter and Prissy were expecting a nice crowd.

Peter reached up to the top shelf of his pantry and pulled down a small brown box. The contents rattled and clinked as he shook it.

He then brought out his rolling pin, recipe card, and cookie sheets. After examining the recipe, he carefully measured, poured, mixed, and stirred.

CHRISTMAS SUGAR COOKIES

Cream with a mixer:
3 eggs
2 softened sticks of margarine
1 cup of sugar
Add:
1 1/2 tsp. vanilla

2 tsp. baking powder
1/2 tsp. salt
Slowly mix in:
3 1/2 cups of flour
Make sure your measurements are accurate.

Chill dough one hour.
Then, working with 1/4 of the dough at a time roll out to desired thickness on a floured surface. Cut with floured cookie cutters. Bake at 350 degrees, 7 minutes or until golden brown. Icing can be made from powdered sugar mixed with milk. Do not make the icing too runny. You can thicken the icing by adding more powdered sugar or flour. Spoon icing into separate cups and add food coloring. Top the cookies with colored icing and enjoy!

He put the dough in the refrigerator to chill and after an hour everything was ready. He rolled out the dough and checked the clock. The guests would be arriving any minute.

Prissy busied herself in the living room at the old rolltop desk. The cookies wouldn't be complete without the special gift tags. She wrote out each tag with care and then cut the edges with shaping scissors. She punched a hole in each on the top left corner and through the hole she strung a brightly colored ribbon.

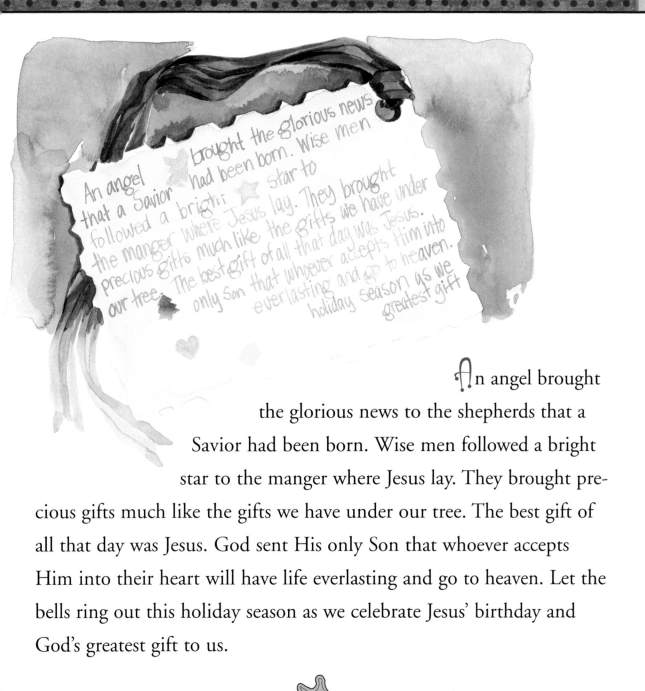

An angel brought the glorious news that a Savior had been born. Wise men followed a bright star to the manger where Jesus lay. They brought precious gifts much like the gifts we have under our tree. The best gift of all that day was Jesus. only Son that whoever accepts Him into everlasting and go to heaven. holiday season as we greatest gift

An angel brought the glorious news to the shepherds that a Savior had been born. Wise men followed a bright star to the manger where Jesus lay. They brought precious gifts much like the gifts we have under our tree. The best gift of all that day was Jesus. God sent His only Son that whoever accepts Him into their heart will have life everlasting and go to heaven. Let the bells ring out this holiday season as we celebrate Jesus' birthday and God's greatest gift to us.

The first guests to arrive were the Warners. Suzy bounded inside Peter's home as energetic as ever, followed by a cheerful Mrs. Warner. Soon Peter and Prissy's home was filled with laughter and excitement as the children gathered around their large oak table and waited for Peter to begin.

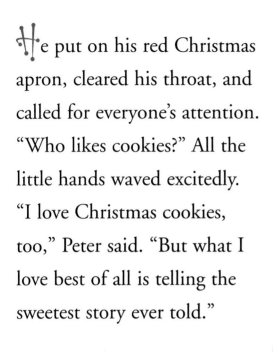

He put on his red Christmas apron, cleared his throat, and called for everyone's attention. "Who likes cookies?" All the little hands waved excitedly. "I love Christmas cookies, too," Peter said. "But what I love best of all is telling the sweetest story ever told."

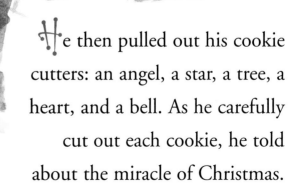

He then pulled out his cookie cutters: an angel, a star, a tree, a heart, and a bell. As he carefully cut out each cookie, he told about the miracle of Christmas.

"An angel brought the glorious news to the shepherds that a Savior had been born."

"Wise men followed a bright star to the manger where Jesus lay."

"They brought precious gifts much like the gifts we have under our tree."

"The best gift of all that day was Jesus. God sent His only Son that who-ever accepts Him into their heart will have life everlasting and go to heaven."

"Let the bells ring out this holiday season as we celebrate Jesus' birthday and God's greatest gift to us."

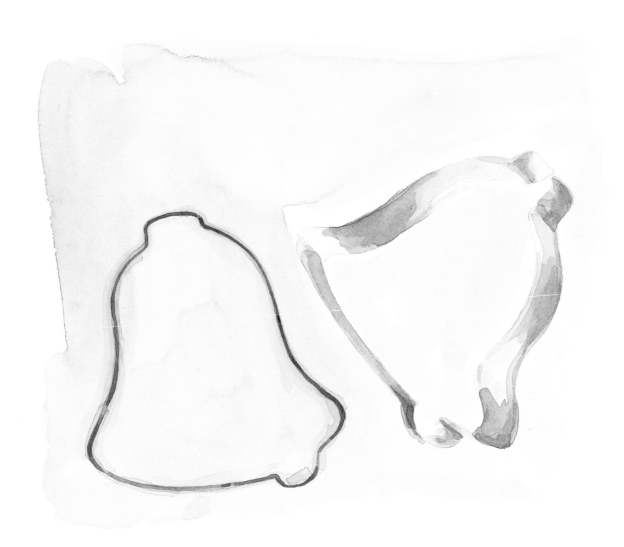

Peter then handed the cookie
cutters to the children and encouraged
them to practice telling the special story
as they cut out cookies. Prissy lifted each cookie
onto metal baking sheets, and soon the wonderful
smell of sugar cookies filled the kitchen.

After the cookies had been baked and
cooled, Prissy brought out candies and bowls
full of colorful icing to decorate the
cookies. Suzy spent most of her time
searching out and decorating the
angels. She carefully spread the white
icing over each cookie and then
formed yellow halos on the
top of each angel's head.

Peter and Prissy sat back and admired all the beautiful cookies. They had made these special cookies a part of the Christmas tradition for more than twenty-five years but couldn't think of a time when they were more beautiful than today.

$\mathcal{S}$oon it was time to bundle up the cookies. They took one of each shape and packaged them up with clear plastic wrap. Then Prissy tied each bundle with the colorful ribbons and tags she'd prepared. Peter then gave each child a bundle to enjoy with their family and three to give away to anyone they felt would benefit from the Christ-centered Christmas goodies. The guests all thanked Peter and Prissy for the wonderful party and left eager to pass out their colorful treasures.

The last guests to leave were the Warners. Mrs. Warner told Peter and Prissy that this holiday gathering was the most special she had ever attended. As Prissy hugged little Suzy, Peter handed Mrs. Warner a small brown box tied with a red-and-white-striped ribbon. "Special delivery from my heart to your home," Peter whispered.

As Mrs. Warner accepted the gift, its contents clinked and rattled. She didn't have to guess what might be inside.

Now Suzy would get that special package she'd been looking for, thanks to Peter and Prissy.

The Warners never forgot the wonderful gift Peter gave them.
Every year they pulled out the special brown box and passed on
the Christmas cookie tradition and the sweetest story ever told.